Our School Orchestra

Sally Cowan

Photographs by Lindsay Edwards

Contents

Playing Music Together

There is an orchestra at my school.

The school orchestra is a large group of children who play music together. They play many kinds of instruments.

I play the violin in the school orchestra. Every week, we practise playing music so that we can perform in concerts.

Learning an Instrument

Children must be learning how to play an instrument before they can join the school orchestra.

Once a week, I have a violin lesson.
I learn how to play the violin,
and how to read music.
The music shows me what **notes** to play
and how many **beats** to count.

It is important for me to practise
playing my violin every day.

Andante
Allegro
Presto
A B A

Instruments in the School Orchestra

There are many kinds of instruments in our orchestra.

Children who play the same kinds of instruments sit together in groups. The main groups are string, wind and percussion.

The instruments in these groups have their own special sounds.

The string instruments have thin strings that are stretched along the "neck" of each instrument.
String instruments make sounds when the strings are moved.

To play my violin, I press the strings down with my fingers.
Then, I move the bow gently backwards and forwards on the strings.

Guitars are bigger string instruments. The guitar players **strum** or **pluck** the strings with their fingers.

The cello (say: *chell-o*) is a string instrument that looks like a huge violin.

The wind instruments make sounds when air is blown into them.

Some of the wind instruments in our orchestra are recorders, flutes and clarinets.
There are trumpets and horns, too.

A recorder is a wind instrument.

To play wind instruments, the players cover the little holes, or press buttons, with their fingers. At the same time, they blow air into their instruments.

A French horn player blows air and presses buttons at the same time.

The percussion instruments make sounds when they are hit, shaken or banged together.

Some children play hand drums, triangles and tambourines in our orchestra.
There are two big xylophones (say: *zy-lo-fones*), too.

My friend Ruby plays the triangle.
It makes a high, ringing sound
when she hits it.

Orchestra Practice

We have orchestra practice twice a week.

Our music teacher, Ms Lowe, is the **conductor**. She stands at the front of the orchestra.

When we play music together,
we watch Ms Lowe carefully.
She shows us when to start and stop
playing our instruments.

Music for the School Orchestra

We play all kinds of music in our orchestra.

Sometimes, we play pop songs.
They can be fast and exciting to play.

Often, Ms Lowe asks us to clap the **rhythm** of a song before we play it. This is a good way to learn how fast or how slowly we need to play our instruments.

We play **classical music**, too.
A lot of classical music is quite old.
People have been playing it
for hundreds of years.

This music can be hard to play,
but Ms Lowe is always ready to help us.

It sounds wonderful
when we all play our **parts**.

Double Bass
Cello

Ms Lowe says that music can tell a story,
just like a book.

My favourite classical music is called
"Peter and the Wolf".
The music tells the story of a boy
who tries to save his animal friends
from a hungry wolf.
The instruments make sounds that remind us
of the noises the animals make,
or of how the animals move around.

The instrument for Peter is the violin,
and the instrument for the wolf is the French horn.
The instruments for the cat, bird and duck
are the clarinet, the flute and the oboe.

School Concerts

Sometimes, the school orchestra performs in concerts at the school hall.

People of all ages come to hear us play.

I like seeing my friends and family
among the people in the hall.
They clap and cheer for the orchestra.

Playing music together in our orchestra
is very exciting.

Glossary

beats (*noun*) steady counts in music

classical music (*noun*) music that is very old

conductor (*noun*) the person who leads an orchestra

notes (*noun*) musical sounds, or the marks used to write them down

parts (*noun*) the music that each instrument makes when played

pluck (*verb*) to give a quick flick or pull with the fingers

rhythm (*noun*) the repeated pattern of short and long sounds in music

strum (*verb*) to move the fingers up and down over the strings